Hurry Home, Grandma!

Hurry Home, Grandma!

by Arielle North Olson · illustrated by Lydia Dabcovich

E. P. DUTTON · NEW YORK

Text copyright © 1984 by Arielle North Olson
Illustrations copyright © 1984 by Lydia Dabcovich

Published in the United States by E. P. Dutton, Inc.,
2 Park Avenue, New York, N.Y. 10016

Published simultaneously in Canada by
Fitzhenry & Whiteside Limited, Toronto

Editor: Ann Durell   Designer: Riki Levinson

Printed in Hong Kong by South China Printing Co.

10 9 8 7 6 5 4 3 2 1   W   First Edition

10374843

Library of Congress Cataloging in Publication Data

Olson, Arielle North.
 Hurry home, Grandma!

 Summary: Timothy and Melinda anxiously anticipate their
explorer grandmother's arrival for Christmas, as she rushes
through various adventures to make it home in time.
 [1. Christmas—Fiction.   2. Grandmothers—Fiction]
I. Dabcovich, Lydia, ill.   II. Title.
PZ7.O51793Hu   1984   [E]   84-1529
ISBN 0-525-44113-1

dedicated to
Mrs. Sterling North
and
Mrs. C. Elmer Olson,
the staunch grandmas
in our family

A. N. O.

for Dorothy

L. D.

"Grandma won't get home in time for Christmas," said Timothy. He licked red and green sugar from his fingers.

"She will too," said Melinda.

Timothy took another cookie and tried to decide what to bite off first—Santa's head or Santa's feet. Melinda ate a reindeer.

"Why did Grandma go exploring anyway?" asked Timothy. "I wish she'd hurry home."

Grandma *was* hurrying—but first she had to chase a monkey who had taken her binoculars.

"Grandma loves to see new places," said
Melinda. She glued some silver glitter on a
pinecone. "But Grandma wouldn't want to miss
Christmas. Nothing will keep her from coming."

Not even crocodiles. But after they chewed
off the end of Grandma's canoe, she had to
paddle pretty hard.

"Scat!" shouted Grandma.

"Grandma wanted to help us decorate the tree," said Timothy, "but Dad says we can't wait any longer. I hope she won't be mad at us."

Grandma *was* mad, but not at Timothy and Melinda.

"Move along now, I'm coming through," she yelled at a group of hippos. "You look clean enough to me."

"Stop! You'll tip over the tree," shouted Melinda. "Anyway, Grandma should decorate the top."

"If this elephant doesn't walk a little faster," said Grandma, "I'm going to be late."

"Look, I finished Grandma's present," said
Timothy. "I wonder what she's bringing us?"

"Let's wrap the presents and put them under
the tree before Grandma gets here," said Melinda.

"If only this plane would make better time,"
said Grandma.

"Hey, Melinda," shouted Timothy. "Here comes Santa Claus!"

"That's not Santa," screamed Melinda. "Here comes Grandma!"

"Timothy, Melinda," cried Grandma.

"I'm home!"

She hugged them both.

"Wow!" said Melinda. "What a great way
to trim a tree."

"Christmas wouldn't be Christmas
without you, Grandma."